The Travellers

The first book:
Tess's story

The second book:
Mike's story

The third book:
Lizzie's story

The Travellers: Mike
by Rosemary Hayes

Published by Ransom Publishing Ltd.
Unit 7, Brocklands Farm, West Meon, Hampshire GU32 1JN, UK
www.ransom.co.uk

ISBN   978 178127 968 7
First published in 2015

Mike

The second book in the series

Rosemary Hayes

Ransom

Acknowledgements

My thanks to everyone who has made time to tell me about the lives of Gypsy/Romany/Travellers, how they live now and how they lived in the past, particularly to those in Cambridgeshire County Council who work with the GRT community and to Gordon Boswell of The Romany Museum, Spalding, Lincolnshire.

I am very grateful to the following members of GRT families who have welcomed me into their homes and talked to me about their experiences:

Brady
Linda
Andrew
Rene
Jessie
Abraham
Abi
and Rita.

The English gypsies I spoke to referred to themselves as either gypsies or travellers, and these terms appear to be interchangeable. Many have Romany roots and still practise some of the old traditions and use words from the Romany language.

Traveller Organisations

The Community Law Partnership (CLP) incorporates the Travellers' Advice Team, a nationwide 24-hour advice service for gypsies and travellers.

The National Federation of Gypsy Liaison Groups

The Gypsy Council

Friends, Families and Travellers

National Association of Gypsy and Traveller Officers

Travellers' Times

The story so far ...

Mike is a gypsy boy of 16. At school he is taunted by his classmates, so he often stays at home. There are family money problems and when Mike and his cousin Johnny are offered cash to do a job for a gang of thieves, they agree, but they are caught. They are let off with a caution because a policeman from a travelling family speaks up for them.

Mike's dad, George, is a horse dealer but, to earn more money, he's gone to work up North for a few months, for his brother Lash, who runs a scrap yard.

George leaves Mike and Johnny in charge of the horses, but when he hears that Mike's been in trouble with the law, he fetches him and takes him to work for Uncle Lash. They leave Johnny to care for the horses with the help of Tess, a pony-mad gorger (non-gypsy) girl from the village.

Uncle Lash is very successful and lives in a fancy house. George is anxious that he doesn't find out that Mike's been in trouble with the law.

One night, George has a phone called from Tess. She's sure that one of the ponies, Flame, whose life she helped to save, will make a show jumper. She wants to train her with the help of the lady from the local riding school.

One

It was the next morning before George told Mike about Tess's phone call. They were just setting off for the scrap yard.

'A show jumper!' Mike stared at his dad. 'We never had jumpers before. Why would she want to do that?'

George shrugged. 'It's worth a try, boy. I don't want to breed from the mare. Maybe the gorger girl can make something of her.'

Mike frowned. He missed the horses – and he

even missed the gorger kid. There were no horses at Lash's place. It was very different up here in Derbyshire. The land was owned by his uncle, and Mike and his dad were living there in their old van. It was shabby, not like the rest – the shiny big vans with the fancy 4x4s to pull them.

'Come on lad, time to go.' George was revving the engine of their old truck. Mike jumped in and they drove the two miles to the scrap yard. Mike hated working there, but he didn't dare complain. He knew exactly what his dad would say.

'You're lucky you're not in jail, boy, after what you did. Keep your head down and work for Uncle Lash. We'll be back home in the Spring.'

The Spring seemed a long way off and Mike worried about the horses. Johnny didn't care about them that much and the gorger girl, Tess, was only a kid.

They approached the big gates of the scrap yard and Mike sighed. It was hard work, pulling cars and lorries apart with heavy tools, sorting the metal into heaps. Filthy, tiring, non-stop work.

Uncle Lash was in the office, speaking on the phone. He nodded when they arrived and beckoned them to come in. Mike and his dad stood there awkwardly, while Lash finished his conversation. The girl at the desk looked up briefly, then went back to staring at her computer screen.

Mike glanced at his dad. Uncle Lash often made them wait, showing he was doing them a favour, giving them work just because they were family. It made George mad, the way he treated them.

At last, Lash switched off his phone. 'Crane driver's off today. Can you work the crane, George?'

George nodded. 'It's bin a while,' he muttered. 'You'll have to show me … '

Lash put his phone in his pocket. 'Come on, then,' he said, and George and Mike followed him out of the office and into the yard.

Mike looked around him. It was dirty and ugly and noisy. On the ground were pools of rainwater, shiny with oil. Everywhere there were heaps of scrap metal and, as he watched, another low loader drove through the gates with its cargo of beaten-up cars.

Uncle Lash called over his shoulder.

'Mike, you can work on that lot.' He pointed to the loader.

Mike nodded. He collected the heavy duty gloves, ingrained with grease, from the store, and the tools he needed, then he walked over to the loader.

The cars bounced and crashed into each other as they came off the loader and Mike and another guy set to work.

Everything came out of the cars – the dashboard, the radio, the wiring, the steering wheel, the tyres, wheels, the bumpers ... every part was added to its correct pile. Even nuts and bolts were put in a special container.

Mike was working beside a big man called Bret. Mike had trouble understanding his accent.

'You family?' asked Bret, when they stopped for a tea break.

Mike nodded. 'Lash is me uncle. Me dad's brother.'

Bret stirred three spoonfuls of sugar into his tea. 'He's done good.'

'Yeah, I s'pose.'

'Not as easy as it was, though.'

'Why's that?'

Bret shrugged. 'Rules and that.'

'What rules?'

Bret looked down at the tea in the polystyrene cup and blew on it.

'Used to be all in cash. Now the tax man gets his cut.'

Mike sniffed. 'Lash still does OK, though.'

'Yeah. There's money in scrap all right.'

As they drank their tea, Mike looked up at the crane, unmoving now, while his dad had his tea break, its great jaws dangling open.

He'd like to work the crane; anything would be better than heaving and yanking at metal all day. It would be a good feeling to scoop up the metal, clamp it in the jaws of the crane, swing the arm up and then dump the lot into the waiting containers.

Bret followed his gaze. 'That stuff goes off to China and all sorts,' he said.

'Yeah.' Mike found it difficult to imagine it, but he'd seen the containers loaded and being driven off. He supposed they went on ships across the sea.

'Yeah,' said Bret, again. 'There's money all right.'

Mike looked up sharply. There was something in Bret's voice – and when their eyes met, Mike looked away quickly, then he pulled on his gloves, picked up a wrench and starting attacking another useless car.

On their way back to the site in the evening, Mike and George bought a takeaway.

A few times they'd eaten with Uncle Lash and his family. Lash had a great shiny new van, gleaming with chrome, and a 4x4 to tow it, but

Lash and his family lived in a house. Everything about it was flash – the brickwork, bright red and new, the fancy ironwork on the outside walls and the statues in the garden. Inside it was the same, with a huge TV and sound system and china knick-knacks on every surface. There was a flash bathroom, too, with gold taps; well, they probably weren't real gold, but they were shiny all right.

Mike knew that his dad felt uncomfortable; he did, too. It was good of Lash to give them a job, but they felt what they were – the poor relations.

Mike was exhausted. Lash had said they could use the bathroom in the house, but they didn't like to and they made do with washing at the sink in the van. Mike's whole body ached from his day's work. He'd never get used to it.

They sat in their van eating their fish and chips.

'Are you finding the work any easier, lad?' asked George.

Mike shook his head.

George sighed. 'I know it's hard, boy. It's hard enough work for a grown man, let alone a lad like you, but Lash pays us well.'

Mike took a mouthful of chips and stared at the ground.

'I just wish we didn't have to … '

'I know. I'm not happy about it, watching Lash show me how he's the big man, making money.'

'How does he do it, Dad?'

'What d'you mean?'

'How can he run the place when he can't read?'

George laughed. 'You don't need book learning to run a scrap yard, boy!'

'But the accounts and stuff.'

George poured more salt on his fish. 'His boys can read and there's that girl in the office and Auntie Lil; she's a scholar. And he's canny. He knows where every penny goes. No one gets one over on Lash.'

'But he ain't no good with horses,' said Mike.

George grinned. 'No, never was. It was always me and me dad that loved the horses.'

He leant over and patted Mike's shoulder. 'And you, son.'

For the rest of the evening they talked about the horses, what they would do with them at the horse fairs later in the year.

And they talked about the chestnut mare, Flame, and whether she might make a show jumper – and about the gorger kid.

Two

The next day, Mike tried to avoid Bret, but it wasn't easy.

'Heard you got into trouble with the law,' he said, as they wrenched and banged at an old car.

Mike's whole body tensed. How had Bret found out? He and Dad hadn't told Uncle Lash.

'What was it – nicking stuff, or what?'

'What are you on about?'

'Don't play the innocent with me, Mikey boy. I got my sources. A little bird told me.'

Mike gripped the wrench tight. 'Leave it, Bret. It was a mistake, OK.'

'Tell yer uncle about it, did yer?'

Mike didn't answer.

'Thought not. He wouldn't be too pleased, would he, if he knew his nephew was a thief?'

Mike said nothing. He turned his back, but he could sense the smirk on Bret's face and he struck out at the heap of old rusted metal in front of him with unnecessary force.

How could Bret know about that business? Had he got some dodgy contact down South? Did he know the gang that had got Mike and Johnny into trouble?

Bret's words scared Mike. He really didn't want his Uncle Lash to know what had happened. Lash was a wheeler-and-dealer, Mike knew that, but Lash kept to the right side of the law – he had to – and if he knew about Mike's trouble, he'd send him packing, and his dad with him. And then Lash would have another reason to look down on them. Not only was Dad less successful than Lash, but he had a thieving son, too.

Bang, bang, bang. Mike scowled, imagining Bret's head underneath the blows of the hammer. Uncle Lash came up behind him.

'You're fair belting that metal, boy.'

Mike jumped.

'Sorry,' said Mike, putting down the hammer and stretching. 'I didn't hear you.'

Uncle Lash beckoned Bret over. He had to yell to make himself heard above the noise in the yard.

'Got a job for you, Bret,' said Lash. 'Take the truck and load it up with those batteries over there.' He pointed at a heap of batteries lying close to one of the skips. 'I can't get much for them and there's that dealer on the other side of town. He's got a contact. He'll take them off me.'

Bret nodded and his face split into a grin showing two broken teeth in his mouth. 'Sure, boss,' he said.

'And take Mike with you. It'll be quicker to unload with the two of you.'

'Nah, I can manage boss,' said Bret.

Uncle Lash frowned. 'You'll do as I say, Bret,' he said. 'It'll be quicker with two and I don't want to pay you overtime.'

Lash started walking away, then he stopped and looked back. 'You hurry up, Bret. The other yard'll be closed by the time you get there, but they'll leave someone to let you in. They've got a guy coming for the batteries tomorrow morning first thing.'

Bret picked up his tools and walked off towards the barn. Mike trailed after him. When they reached the barn, Bret slammed down the tools on the bench, took a set of keys from a hook, got into a truck and fired the engine. He crashed the gears and roared out of the barn and into the yard, without waiting for Mike.

When Mike caught up with him, Bret was scowling with fury.

'I can manage on my own,' he muttered. 'I don't need no scrawny kid with me.'

Mike said nothing. Then suddenly Bret turned to him, that sly expression on his face again.

'Tell you what, Mikey boy,' he said. 'Why don't you go over to the office and get us both a cuppa. I'll start the loading.'

Mike was puzzled. They'd not long had their tea break.

'OK,' he said.

He walked away slowly. He turned back once and saw that Bret was watching him.

There were some of the other workers helping themselves from the tea dispensing machine, so it was a while before Mike got back to Bret.

'Good lad,' said Bret, smiling. 'Now, you hand me the batteries – one at a time, they're heavy old things – and I'll stack 'em in the back of the truck.

It took a long time. There were a lot of batteries in the heap. Mike picked them from the pile, one by one, and handed them over to Bret to load in the truck. They were much heavier than they looked and by the time they had finished Mike was sweating with the effort and his arms and back ached. As the last one went in, Bret hurriedly drew the canvas cover over the back of the truck.

Mike noticed that Bret hadn't touched his tea.

'You sure you want to come, lad? I could drop you off at your van on the way?'

'No. I'd better come. You heard what Lash said.'

Bret frowned and gunned the engine. 'Always do what yer uncle says, do you, Mike? Scared of him are you?'

Mike didn't answer, but he clenched his fists at his sides as they drove off.

It was slow getting to the other yard. They had to drive through the town and then out several miles the other side, but Bret seemed in no hurry. By the time they reached the yard it was almost dark.

'Hope there's some lights there,' said Mike, the first words he'd said on the journey.

'No need for light,' said Bret shortly. 'I know where they want the stuff put.'

They drove through the gates.

'It's smaller than our yard,' said Mike, looking about him.

'*Ours* now, is it?'

'Lash's.'

Bret cleared his throat. Then he opened the window and spat out a great blob of phlegm onto the ground, before driving into the middle of the yard and parking near some skips. After a while, when no one came, he got out of the truck and sauntered over to a shed a little way off, whistling, his hands in his pockets.

A few minutes later, he came back with another man. The other man peered into the truck.

'Who's this, then?' he asked, pointing at Mike.

'The kid? He's Lash's nephew.'

Mike couldn't see the other man's face but he could sense his anger.

'What's he doing here?'

'Don't worry about young Mike,' said Bret. 'He's just along for the ride.'

'I'm supposed to help,' said Mike, struggling out of the passenger seat, every muscle hurting.

Bret pushed him back. 'You take a rest, lad,' he said. 'I got a helper now. We'll soon have this unloaded.'

Mike sank thankfully back into the seat. He wasn't going to argue.

He listened as the men heaved the batteries into the waiting skip, grunting and swearing. Mike drew his jacket round him and hunkered down into the seat. His eyes drooped and he began dozing off.

Suddenly he was jerked awake by a loud yell. He yanked open the door and jumped out of the van.

By the edge of the skip, Bret was standing over the other man, who was jumping up and down on one leg. Mike saw immediately what had happened. The other guy had dropped a battery on his toe. Ouch!

Bret had whirled round when he heard the door open.

'No harm done,' he shouted. 'Get back in the truck.'

Mike nodded, but just as he turned to get in again, he saw something that made his heart race.

Most of the batteries had been unloaded and now he could see that there was something else in the truck, something that until now had been covered up.

Copper tubing. As soon as Mike saw it, he turned quickly away.

But not quickly enough. Bret had seen him looking at it.

Three

Mike sat in the car and listened to Bret and the other man talking together in low voices, as they continued unloading. He heard his name mentioned and his stomach clenched. He wished he'd not seen that tubing. He guessed at once what Bret was up to. He was stealing from Uncle Lash. He and his companion were selling stuff on the side.

At last Bret opened the driver's door. He stuffed some money into the back pocket of his jeans and got in.

As they drove away, Bret glanced at Mike a couple of times, but he didn't say anything. Then when he dropped Mike off at the van and Mike made to open the door, Bret gripped his arm.

'You didn't see anything back there, did you Mikey boy?'

Mike shook his head. 'No,' he muttered.

Bret tightened his grip. 'Good,' he said. 'Our little secret, eh?'

Mike nodded.

'Good,' said Bret again. Then he added, ''Cos you wouldn't like yer uncle to know about the spot of bother you had down South, would you?'

Mike shook his head.

At last Bret released him. 'See you in the morning then.'

Mike felt sick as he walked to the van. His dad was already there, washing his grimy hands and face in the tiny basin. He turned as Mike came in and smiled at him, but Mike didn't return his smile.

George finished washing. 'You OK, son?'

Mike nodded. 'Just tired.'

George went out to get a takeaway and Mike cleaned himself up. He ought to tell Lash what was going on. He knew he should. But if he grassed on

Bret, then Bret would tell Lash that Mike had been in trouble with the law.

As they were eating their dinner, Mike asked, 'How much longer will we be here, Dad?'

George took a long sup of his can of beer. He wiped his lips with the back of his hand.

'We'll get back soon. Once the better weather comes, I can help Johnny's dad with the gardening work. And we'll need to get the horses ready for the fairs, too.'

The horses.

Mike took out his phone. 'I'm going to phone Tess. See how she's getting on.'

'She's OK, that gorger kid,' said George, grinning. 'She'll see to them.'

'Better than Johnny,' muttered Mike.

Tess wasn't picking up when he phoned. He checked his watch. She'd be down at the field filling the haynets and checking the water, talking to the horses, patting them, whispering to them. He sighed. He could almost smell them, that special horsey scent that was so much a part of him.

He got through later. He wasn't much good at talking. Like his dad, he only said what needed saying, but Tess talked enough for both of them.

She gave him a breathless rundown on each one of the ponies in turn.

'What about Flame – and her foal?' asked Mike.

Tess's voice softened. 'You know what, Mike, I think you've got a real jumper there.'

'Yeah?'

Tess hesitated. 'You know your dad said I could get the lady from the riding school to look at her?'

'Yeah.'

'Well, she came at the weekend and brought a few little jumps and we lunged Flame over them.'

'You shouldn't do that. Not til her foal's weaned!'

'It's OK. We were really careful. You should have seen her Mike, she seemed to know just what to do.'

Mike didn't reply.

'I promise I won't let anything happen to her.'

'Yeah. I know. Thanks. How's Johnny? Has he been helping?'

There was a brief silence, then, 'Well, he's been busy up at the Tech, Mike.'

'So that's a *no* then?'

'It's hard for him. He's tired when he gets back.'

'*He's* tired! He should try bashing metal all day, then he'd know about *tired*.'

'How's it going up there?'

Mike sighed. "S'orright, I s'pose. The money's not bad. But we miss the horses. Me uncle's not like Dad. He lives in this fancy house and he's got this big yard. He's never bothered about horses.'

'Everything OK?' asked George, when Mike was off the phone.

Mike nodded. 'She's doing it all herself, Dad.'

'She's a good lass.'

'Johnny should be helping her.'

George nodded. 'He's wasting his time up at the Tech. He won't learn nothing his dad can't teach him.'

The Tech had offered Mike a practical course, too, but there was nothing he fancied. There were gardening courses and bricklaying courses – Johnny was doing the bricklaying – but Mike knew what he wanted to do. He wanted to work with horses, but he didn't want to be like his dad, scratching a living from this and that. A bit of horse dealing, some gardening work, doing stuff for family.

George stretched. 'When I was a kid, you didn't need no bits of paper to show what you could do. We didn't need no qualifications then.'

Mike had heard it all before and he zoned out as

his dad talked about his time growing up in the fens, where all the kids worked on the land from the time they were eight or nine years old, picking peas, potatoes, leeks, then going on to soft fruit.

'There weren't any chance of schooling then, boy. Your life's soft now.'

Mike looked down at his calloused hands. It didn't seem soft.

'And you can read an' all. Not like me and your mam.'

'Mam can. A bit. She learnt from our school books.'

George smiled. 'She's a hard worker, your mam. She could've bin a scholar if she'd had the chance.'

But instead she's cleaning offices, thought Mike. But he kept quiet.

'I'm off to bed, Dad. I'm knackered.'

Mike drew the curtain across his part of the van and crawled into bed, but he lay awake for a long time, listening to his dad talking on the phone. Mike wondered who he was speaking to.

But that wasn't all that kept him awake. Even though he was dead tired and every muscle ached, he kept seeing the copper lying in the bottom of the truck.

And when he finally dropped off to sleep, he

had a nightmare about Bret. Bret and his companion chasing him, shouting at him, brandishing a length of copper piping and getting closer and closer until ...

He woke with a start to find his dad standing over him, shaking him.

'You're shouting as if the demons are after you lad. What is it? Did you have a bad dream?'

For a moment, Mike stared up at him, still stuck in his nightmare. Then his heart calmed down.

'Yeah. Just a bad dream. Sorry I woke you.'

George grunted and stumbled back to his own bed. But Mike couldn't sleep for the rest of the night. He lay shivering, waiting for the dawn to break, dreading the next day.

Four

As they were driving to the yard the next morning, George suddenly cleared his throat.

'I bin offered some work abroad,' he announced. He didn't look at Mike, but continued to stare at the road ahead.

So that was what that long phone call last night had been about.

Mike turned and looked at him. 'What work? Where?'

'The cousins that went working in Europe last

year; they're going again and they want me to go with them.'

'Will you go?'

George shrugged. 'Told them I'll think about it.'

Mike said nothing.

'They made good money there,' said George at last. 'Steady work all season. Tarmac spreading, fruit picking, then there's the cousins that go round market trading, picking up antiques and that.'

'Better than the gardening?'

'Yeah.'

'But ... '

George glanced across at Mike. 'I know, son. It's the horses. I don't want to leave the horses. And if I go, I'd have to leave next month.'

'You'd miss out on the fairs, then.'

He nodded. 'What do you reckon, Mike? Could you and Johnny manage the horses while I'm gone?'

'Johnny won't do much,' muttered Mike.

'Johnny's dad could drive you to the horse fairs, help with the selling and that.'

'And the gorger kid,' said Mike. 'She could help.'

For a moment, George hesitated. 'Yeah, maybe,' he said at last. 'But she's not one of us.'

Mike looked up. 'She's bin a sight more help

than Johnny. She's bin doing all the work while we've bin up here.'

'I know.' George sighed. 'But be careful, son. You don't want to get her involved in the horse dealing, that's not her place. She don't understand our ways. She can't, can she?'

Mike said nothing and they were silent until they reached the yard.

It was a bright sunny day but very cold and, as he worked, Mike could see his breath in clouds of moisture in front of his face. By the end of the morning, his fingers and toes were numb. His dad found him and handed him a mug of soup and a sandwich; they walked over to the office together and stood in the warm.

Bret joined them and Mike immediately felt nervy, scared he might say something to his dad.

If Dad goes to Europe, then we'll have to leave soon and Bret will be off my back.

He grinned at the thought. No more being grateful to Uncle Lash or being scared of what Bret might say.

Bret slurped down his soup noisily and wiped his mouth with the back of his hand.

'Come on, lad,' he said. 'We've got another delivery to make.'

Mike stopped smiling. He didn't want to be in the truck with Bret. He didn't want to make a delivery with him.

'Can't you manage on yer own?'

Bret glanced across at George. 'Not keen, is he, yer son?'

George frowned. 'Go on, Mike. You heard what Bret said.'

As they roared out of the yard, Bret turned to Mike. 'We're meeting a friend of mine,' he said.

Mike's stomach clenched. 'Don't we have to deliver this load?'

'Yeah, but it's daytime, isn't it? Got to offload something special first. '

Mike said nothing. They were driving up a side road now, well away from the main traffic. Bret drew off the road and parked in a layby, turned off the engine and took out his phone. 'We're here,' he said, then he snapped the phone shut and sat back in his seat, whistling tunelessly.

Moments later, another truck roared up the road and came to a halt just behind them. Bret jumped out.

A different man this time.

How many of them are in this scam?

Again, the man pointed to Mike and Mike saw Bret laugh and slap the other guy on the back. Something was transferred from the back of their truck to the other one, then, with a last glance at Mike, the guy got into his truck and drove off.

Bret got back into the driving seat. Again, he was stuffing some notes into his back pocket, but he kept one back and held it out to Mike.

''Ere you are, lad. A tenner for keeping yer trap shut.'

Mike felt the fury rise in him. He batted the note away.

Bret's eyes narrowed. 'Please yerself,' he said. 'It's all the same to me.' Then, as they drove off, he said, 'If you grass on me, son, you'll know about it.'

Mike nodded. He knew it was a threat.

When they reached the other yard, there were lots of people around. Mike saw the guy they'd met the other night. He nodded at Mike.

Silently, Mike helped Bret unload more batteries and other small items that Lash didn't deal in, then they headed back.

How many more trips would Bret involve him in? It was as if he wanted Mike to know just how much he was cheating Uncle Lash.

The longer this goes on, the harder it will be for me to tell anyone. I should have told Dad that first time. And what did Bret mean when he said, 'You'll know about it'? Would he send someone to beat him up, threaten him?

That evening, George was on the phone again. This time he talked about the calls with Mike.

'I've had a word with Johnny's dad,' he said. 'And he's happy to drive the horse box to the fairs and he'll take you on, too. He wants you to help with the gardening, seeing as I won't be there and Johnny's at the Tech.'

'Have you spoken to Mam?' asked Mike.

For a moment, his dad frowned. 'Yeah,' he said briefly.

Mike didn't push it. He could imagine what Mam had said. Mam wanted him to go back to school, take some exams.

He sighed. 'It's all settled then?'

George patted him on the back and smiled. 'Yeah. We'll leave here in a fortnight. I'll tell Lash tomorrow.'

Lash was none too pleased when they told him. George had left it until the evening and for once had accepted Lash's offer of a meal at his house.

As they entered the house, Mike could feel his dad tense up and he, too, cringed as Auntie Lil hugged him, the sweet smell of her perfume making his eyes smart and her bright lipstick leaving a mark on his cheek.

They walked into the lounge, where everything seemed to twinkle at them. Auntie Lil was keen on pink and everything that wasn't pink was sparkling; glittering mirrors, gilt ornaments. Mike blinked in the bright lights.

Auntie Lil was generous with the food, though, and Mike tucked in, but he noticed that his dad was hardly eating anything.

He's scared of Lash. Scared of what he'll say.

They talked of this and that, of who was doing what in the family, but Mike could see that his dad wasn't really engaged.

Lash had had a beer or two and he was boasting about a holiday he and Lil were going to take in the Canary Islands. Mike had no idea where the Canary Islands were, but they sounded exotic.

'It's good you're here, George,' said Lash. 'I can leave the place in your hands while we're away. It's good to have family here. Someone I can trust.'

Trust! If Uncle Lash knew about Mike's trouble with

the law and that he'd not said anything about Bret's scam, he wouldn't be so keen to trust his family.

Mike could see a vein throbbing at the side of his dad's head and noticed that he was picking nervously at the threads of his old jumper.

'I can't stop, Lash,' he blurted out at last.

'What? What d'you mean you can't stop?'

George swallowed. He was looking really uncomfortable.

He didn't meet Lash's eyes. 'The thing is, I bin offered farm work abroad. It's good money.'

There was a horrible silence, only broken by the ticking of a fancy glass clock on the mantelpiece. Mike glanced at Auntie Lil, who was looking nervously at Lash.

Lash rose slowly to his feet and stood towering over George.

'Still the same old George,' said Lash, his hands on his hips. 'And I thought you'd changed. Thought I could rely on you. How stupid of me.'

'It was only temporary, Lash,' said George quietly. 'I said I could only work with you for a bit.'

'So, I get you out of a hole – again – and as soon as something better comes up, you take off. Typical!'

George's fists were clenched.

Mike looked at his feet, praying that Lash wouldn't rile his dad any more. If it came to a fight, Lash would come off worse.

Five

Somehow they got out of the house without the two men coming to blows, but Lash had said some cruel things and the atmosphere was toxic.

And he'd told them to go immediately, said he couldn't stand the sight of George or his 'no-good son' any longer and they were to leave his land by morning. Then the atmosphere got even worse when George insisted he be paid up to date, and there was a lot of shouting until Auntie Lil, her face set hard, had left the room and returned with cash which she slapped into George's hand.

'Count it if you like,' she said, standing over him with her arms folded.

But he put it in his pocket without looking at it. 'Thanks Lil.'

George and Mike walked back to their van. Mike didn't dare say anything until his dad broke the silence.

'He's a tough one, your Uncle Lash,' he said, rubbing his hands together and blowing on them. 'Sweet as pie when everything's going his way, but it doesn't do to rile him.'

Mike said nothing. If Uncle Lash found out about Bret's scam, what then? Would he connect it with Mike? If he did, then that would rile him for sure.

His dad went on. 'Just the same when we were kids. He was always the one who got what he wanted, wheedling and charming. But he's a good businessman, I'll give him that.'

It didn't take them long, the next morning, to pack up the van. Soon they were driving south. The sun came out and it was a frosty clear day. Mike's spirits rose. No more Bret. No more threats. And he didn't feel so bad, now, for not telling Uncle Lash about the scam. It had probably been going on for months anyway. Long before he worked at the yard.

It was only a couple of hours' drive, but they stopped at a motorway service station half way and had a big fry up – and George smoked a roll up outside, squinting in the sunshine.

'It'll be good to see the horses again,' he said, stretching.

'Yeah.'

'You all right with that, boy? Doing the horse fairs and that while I'm away?'

Mike hesitated. He thought briefly of what Mr Hardy had said to him about going to the special college at Milton and getting some sort of qualification to work with horses. He looked up at his dad. There'd never be a better moment.

'There's courses at that place in Milton, Dad. Leaning about horses and that.' He went on. 'I'd need to go back to school, get a couple of GCSEs, but Milton's not far from the site. It'd be easy to get there.'

George frowned. Then he laughed and slapped Mike on the back. 'Don't be daft, boy. What could some fancy course teach you? You know a sight more about horses than most.'

Mike shrugged. That was that, then. He'd follow his dad's footsteps. A bit of horse dealing, a bit of gardening, tiling, laying patios. Not such a bad life, he supposed. But he kept hearing Mr Hardy's words in his head. *You're better than that, Mike. You're bright. You could make something of yourself.*

He shrugged. What did he know?

He grinned. 'Yeah,' he said. 'I guess I know more than any fancy horse teacher.'

Soon they were passing the familiar landmarks. Mike turned and stared out of the window, waiting for the first glimpse of their site from the motorway. He always enjoyed looking down from the motorway as it crossed over, high above the site, where you could see the cluster of vans and then the fields beyond with their horses in it, tiny blobs of black and white or brown and white.

There! He saw the site, and then the fields behind it. But they were empty!

'Dad!'

Mike screwed round. 'Dad. The horses!'

'Eh?'

'They're not there!'

'What?'

'The horses. They're not in the field.'

George frowned. He glanced quickly down, across the motorway lanes, in the direction of the site, but they had already passed it.

'They must be there, son. It's a biting cold day. They'd be hunkered against the hedge.'

Mike bit his lip, a horrible feeling in the pit of his stomach. He knew where to look. He knew where they'd be. And there were no horses there.

What's happened to them?

But he kept quiet, his fists clenched against his side, until they drove off at the next exit. The next half mile stretched for ever. Every set of traffic lights was red, his dad seemed in no hurry, humming now, looking forward to being back home, smiling.

I'm right. I know I'm right. They're not there.

At last they drove past the college, under the motorway, along the potholed road and into the site. As they slowed down to drive in, Mike opened the passenger door.

'I'll just check on the horses,' he said.

George grinned. 'Can't even wait to see your mam first, eh?'

But Mike was gone, running down the lane which led to the field at the back, slipping on the frosty mud, still hard in places where the sun couldn't reach it, shaded by the high hedge. Then round the corner which led to the gate. He vaulted the gate, but his hands slipped on the wet iron railing and he went flying, landing heavily on the ground and twisting his ankle. He picked himself up, swearing and biting back the tears of pain, but ran on across the field, calling the names of the horses.

There was not a sound in response. No thudding of hooves, no neighing, nothing.

In the middle of the field he stopped and put his hands on his knees, getting his breath back and relieving the pain in his side. He hardly noticed the throbbing pain in his ankle as he raised his head and looked all round the field, into the dark shady patches near the hedges, in the shelter in the corner.

Nothing. They were all gone.

He tried to fight the panic and looked carefully at the fencing. It had never been great, but the horses had never tried to get out. He started to limp around the edge of the field, his ankle hurting and his breath short.

And then he saw it. Two of the fence posts lying on the ground, the tangled barbed wire a lethal heap between them. And the tell-tale hoof prints either side, sharply defined in the frosty mud.

The horses had broken through the gap, through the hedge and onto the lane.

And then where?

And why had no one noticed? How long had they been gone?

He doubled back, running down the lane as fast as he could, trying to ignore the pain in his ankle, arriving at their van just as the family had gathered around his dad.

'Mike!' said his mam, coming to hug him. But she never got there. His dad immediately knew that something was wrong and came forward.

'What's happened, lad?'

'They've gone!' gasped Mike. 'The horses. They've all gone – broken through the fence!'

Mike had seen his dad angry before, but never like this. He yelled at Mam, yelled at the other children, yelled at Mike.

'Where's Johnny?'

'At the Tech,' muttered Mam.

'At the Tech! What's the use of that?'

He rounded on Mike then. 'And that gorger girl. What were you thinking of, getting friendly with her sort, she's … she's … ' He spat on the ground.

Mike said nothing.

George shouted at him. 'Fetch some headcollars and ropes and get in the truck,' he said.

By this time some of the other families had gathered.

'What are you gawping at?' He pointed at a couple of teenage lads. 'You two, come and help.'

George uncoupled the van and, by the time Mike came back with head collars and ropes, his dad was gunning the engine of the truck and had the two other lads sitting in the back.

They drove off, scattering gravel and flying over the bumpy potholes. Mike took out his phone.

'What are you doing?'

'Phoning Tess,' he said.

Six

Tess wasn't picking up. Mike swore under his breath. Of *course*, she'd be at school, in lessons.

He left a message. 'Tess. It's Mike. The horses are gone. Phone me.'

George glanced across at him but said nothing.

After that there was silence. Mike and the other boys could all sense George's fury and they kept quiet.

By now, others from the site had heard what had happened and there were two cars following them.

George drove slowly, peering from side to side as they made their way up the road past the Tech. He thumped the steering wheel with his fist.

'There's nowhere for them to go,' he muttered. Then he stopped the truck and jumped out. The other cars drew up.

George gave them instructions and they all set off in different directions.

Mike was thinking furiously. His dad was right. Where would the horses go? There was no unfenced land in the village; surely they'd just be grazing on the verges. And surely someone would have seen them?

He broke the silence. 'Dad.'

George grunted.

'We should ask in the village. They'll have bin seen.'

George scowled. 'I don't want the help of no gorger folk.'

Mike swallowed. 'I'll do the asking, Dad. Just pull up at the village shop.'

George didn't answer and Mike thought he would drive past the shop but, at the last moment, he jammed on the brakes, making Mike and the others shunt forward in their seats.

'Be quick about it, then.'

Mike jumped out and ran into the shop. There were several customers in the shop and they all turned to look at him.

''Ave you seen our horses?' he said, breathless. 'They've got loose and we can't find them.'

'Damn gypsies,' muttered someone. But the shopkeeper cleared his throat.

'Can anyone help?' he asked. 'Has anyone seen this lad's horses?'

'They're coloured horses,' said Mike, blushing. 'Black and white and brown and white. Cobs.'

Everyone shook their heads and there was more muttering. Then someone said. 'When did they go missing?'

'I dunno,' said Mike. 'We just got back and saw the fence broken.'

As they were speaking, the post office van drew up outside the shop.

'We could ask the postie,' said the shopkeeper. 'He's been up since dawn. He may have seen something.'

Mike glanced outside. He could see his father in the truck, his fingers drumming impatiently on the steering wheel. The post van was behind the truck and the postman was leaning into it, picking stuff up. Mike walked out to him.

'We've lost our horses,' he said. He gestured back towards the shop. 'They said you might have seen them.'

The postman withdrew his head from his van and stood up.

'Now you mention it,' he said, stroking his chin. 'Yes. I did see a few horses.'

'Where? Where did you see them?'

'It was earlier this morning. Out the other side of the village.' He frowned. 'To be honest, I didn't take much notice. I thought they were tethered.'

'Out the other side?' said Mike. 'Which way?'

The postman pointed. 'That way. Not far from the level crossing.'

Mike felt as though he'd been hit in the stomach.

The level crossing, the gates across a busy line with trains coming and going down the track all the time.

'Thanks,' he muttered, and flung himself into his dad's truck.

'The level crossing,' he said. 'They were seen near the level crossing.'

George looked at him. They didn't exchange a word. They didn't need to. George gunned the engine and they roared off, through the village, past the primary school and the last of the houses.

When they reached the level crossing, there was

no sign of the horses, but there was a track running alongside the railway line. George wrenched the steering wheel round and tried to drive down it, but it was too bumpy and overgrown and he had to stop. He killed the engine and jumped out, grabbed the head collars and ropes and started running down the track.

'Come on,' he yelled to the others, over his shoulder.

They seemed to run for hours, jumping over brambles and tripping on the rutted surface. Adrenaline kept Mike going and he pounded after his dad, even though his ankle hurt. The other lads couldn't keep up and they soon stopped running, puffing and panting with effort, and slowed to a walk.

'It's no good, Dad. They're not here!' gasped Mike, as they both stopped for a moment to draw breath.

George turned and grabbed Mike by the shoulders. 'We can't lose them, son.'

His eyes were wild and his chest heaved.

'We'll find them, Dad,' said Mike.

He wished he believed it.

Suddenly Mike's phone rang. He fished it out of his pocket. It was Tess.

'Where are you Mike? What's happened?'

'Dad and I came back this morning. The horses are gone.'

'You're back? But I thought ... '

Mike cut her off, his voice harsh. 'Never mind. We're out looking for them now. I can't talk.'

'Where? Where are you looking?'

'By the railway track,' Mike said shortly and he heard her sharp intake of breath.

'I'm coming,' she said.

'What?'

'I'm on my way.'

'What do you mean? You're at school.'

But she'd hung up.

I hope she doesn't turn up. Dad's angry and he won't hold back. She's never seen his temper.

The other lads caught them up and together the group of them forged on, stopping every now and again to look around them.

'How long does this path go on?' asked Mike.

George shrugged. 'Dunno.'

About ten minutes later, they had their answer. The path petered out and beyond it was a patch of wasteland.

Suddenly, one of the other lads shouted.

'Look! Up in them trees!'

George screwed up his eyes and stared in the direction of the lad's pointing finger. 'What? Where? I can't see nothing.'

'There's summat moving in them trees,' said the lad.

Mike was looking, too. 'He's right, Dad.'

But George wasn't convinced.

'More likely deer,' he mumbled.

'Let's go and see,' said Mike. And before his dad could answer, he was running across the wasteland, up the steep slope that led towards the small outcrop of trees. As he came closer, he could see more clearly. He was well ahead of the others and he turned round.

'It's them!' he shouted. 'They're here.'

His whole body was flooded with relief and he found that he was shaking as he approached the trees.

He called to the horses softly as he came closer, naming each one. He put his hand in his pocket and brought out some carrots. The other hand was behind his back, holding a head collar.

One of the horses raised its head and whinnied, trotting towards him. Mike stood completely still, the carrot in the flat of his hand, waiting patiently. Behind him, George and the others stopped, too, knowing not to scare the animals.

It was one of the older cobs that had broken free from the herd.

If I can get a head collar on him, the others may follow.

Slowly, the animal approached. He had seen the carrot and he was blowing suspiciously through his nostrils.

'It's me, boy,' said Mike quietly. 'You know me.'

Time seemed to stop as the cob considered his options. Mike shivered with cold. He'd not felt cold before, the running had kept him warm. Now he could feel the cold sweat trickling down his back.

A bird suddenly flapped noisily out of the trees, startling the horse. It put its head up and trotted away, then put its head down and started cropping the grass.

Very slowly, Mike walked towards it, the carrot still in his extended hand.

'Come on, boy,' he said.

The cob raised its head and then, suddenly, it seemed to recognize Mike and it whinnied again.

Mike smiled and continued to walk forward. This time the animal stood still. Mike gave him the carrot and stroked his nose. Then, very slowly, he slipped the head collar over its neck and buckled it.

His dad and the others walked up to him.

'Well done lad,' said George. As Mike led the cob down the hill, the other horses emerged from the trees and started to follow them. One by one, George and the other lads managed to get head collars on them and, by the time they had reached the track by the railway, all the horses were safe.

All except two.

'Where's Flame and her foal?' said Mike.

George grunted. 'We can't go looking for her now. We gotta walk this lot back.'

Seven

As they walked the horses down the hill, Mike spotted a figure in the distance, running down the path beside the railway line.

The gorger girl! Even from a long way away, he recognised her. He glanced at his dad. He'd seen her too.

'What's she doing here?' he said. He turned to Mike. 'Did you tell her to come?'

Mike shook his head. 'No, I ... '

'She's nothing but trouble. I want her away from our horses, do you hear?'

'But Dad, she's been caring for them ... '

'*Caring* for them! How come they've all escaped, then?'

Mike could hear the fury in his dad's voice. He kept quiet.

When Tess spotted them, she stopped running and waved, waiting for them to reach her. She was panting and bent over, her hands on her knees.

Then she stood up and looked more carefully at the group of horses coming towards her. As soon as Mike was within hearing distance, she shouted.

'Where's Flame? Is she safe?'

Mike didn't answer. He was leading three of the horses now and he kept his eyes on the ground ahead. As he came closer, Tess walked towards him. Her face was red and her hair was loose, blowing about in the icy wind.

'What happened? How did they ... ?'

But George, who was beside Mike now, cut in, his face taut with anger.

'Go back, girl,' he said. 'Keep away from my horses, do you hear?'

But Tess stood her ground. 'What do you mean?' she said. 'I've been looking after them all this time.'

George stepped forward so that he was close to her, towering over her.

'Letting them get away. Do you call that looking after them?' His voice was rising dangerously and Mike tried to send a warning glance to Tess. The gorger girl didn't know what his dad was like when he was riled.

But Tess ploughed on, tears springing to her eyes. 'The fencing's always been bad on that field,' she said. 'I kept telling … '

'Telling who?' growled George.

Tess dropped her head. 'Never mind,' she muttered.

Mike looked at her. She was loyal, he'd give her that. She was protecting Johnny. He was willing to bet she'd told Johnny about the dodgy fencing, asked him to do something about it.

'Are all the horses safe now?' she asked. 'Is Flame still back at the site?'

Mike shook his head. 'There weren't no horses in the field,' he said shortly.

Tess grabbed his arm but he shook it off, glancing at his dad.

'We must find her Mike,' she said. 'D'you think she's round here somewhere? '

Mike shrugged.

George interrupted. 'Phone Johnny's dad,' he said to Mike. 'Get him to come with the horse box. We must get this lot back.'

'What about Flame and the foal?' Tess was shouting now. 'You must keep looking for them.'

'*Must*, must I?' George yelled back. 'Giving me orders now, are you?'

Mike could see the colour rising in George's cheeks.

Don't push it, Tess. He'll lash out at you.

Tess didn't answer. She was trying to keep back her tears.

Then there was a shout from one of the other boys and they all turned to look where he was pointing.

Mike gasped and Tess stopped crying and stared up the railway line.

In the distance, just on the bend, they could see it. The tiny figure of Flame's foal, by itself, standing on the railway track.

'NO!' she screamed, and before anyone could stop her she had snatched up a spare rope from Mike and was running up the path, forcing her way through the bramble patches and stumbling on the rutted ground.

For a moment, none of the others moved, then

George handed the horses he was holding to Mike.

'Stay here,' he commanded, and started running after Tess. But George wasn't fit and he was heaving and panting as he chased her. Tess didn't look back and she had reached the point in the path, opposite where the foal stood on the railway line, well before him.

When George caught up with her, she was looking further down the track. She pointed.

'There's Flame,' she gasped. 'Look, she's trying to get to her foal. She's trying to get through onto the railway line.'

George followed her gaze. Sure enough, the mare was thrashing about frantically by the side of railway line, trying to force herself through the barbed wire fence that protected the path from the line.

'How did the foal get through?' muttered George, as he pushed down on the barbed wire and climbed over the fence and onto the line, tearing his hands. But the foal skittered away from him as he approached it.

Then, suddenly, Flame stopped crashing about in the undergrowth beside the line and turned back. George and Tess watched in horror as the mare took a run at the fence. Tess closed her eyes, sure that Flame would be tangled up in the barbed wire, but the next moment she heard a thud and the crunch of pebbles. She opened her eyes.

She had made it! The mare was on the railway line, unharmed and reunited with her foal.

For a second, George stared. Unlike Tess, he had seen it all. Seen how the mare had galloped towards the fence, even in her panic setting herself right at the obstacle in front of her, and soaring over it easily.

Now the foal was beside its mother and they were nuzzling each other. Carefully, George approached them.

'I'll have to try and carry the little 'un,' he said. 'It'll never get back on its own.'

Tess nodded, looking up and down the line to see if there was any break in the fencing. There must be. The foal must have broken through somewhere.

But as she was looking, she saw something else.

'The signal!' she screamed.

George looked up briefly.

'The signal's changed! A train's coming!'

Somehow, George got his arms round the foal, finding some superhuman strength from somewhere, heaved it, struggling and kicking, towards the fence and dropped it over. Then Tess hung onto its mane as it struggled and lashed out at her. George clambered over the barbed wire to help and together they managed to force it to the ground and hold it down.

But Flame was still on the line, rearing up, pounding with her hooves.

'She's got no run up,' gasped Tess. 'She's panicking.'

And then they heard it. The sound of the train in the distance.

Tess loosed her hold on the foal and left George to handle it. Numb to any pain, she clambered over the barbed wire, snagging her clothes and piercing her hands.

By this time, Flame was frantic, pacing up and down, whinnying to her foal, her eyes wide with fright and her nostrils flaring.

The train was coming closer, whistling as it approached the bend on the line.

'Get to the edge or you'll both be killed!' yelled George. He loosed his grip on the foal and it struggled free, throwing itself towards the fence.

Tess kept her eyes on Flame. Suddenly the mare stilled and looked at her.

'It's me, girl,' whispered Tess. 'It's OK.'

She only had seconds before the train would be on them, but in those seconds she managed to throw her arms round the mare's neck, fling her leg over her back and kick her firmly in the flanks as she pointed her towards the fence.

'Please do it girl,' she prayed, clinging on with all her strength.

For a moment the mare hesitated, then she saw her foal batting itself against the fence on the other side and, from a standstill, she gathered herself and jumped, landing neatly on the path.

She dropped her head and nuzzled her foal. Tess was still sitting on her back, her arms round the mare's neck, sobbing. On the other side of the fence, the train roared past them.

George picked up the rope and knotted it round Flame's neck. He didn't ask Tess to dismount, but led them back down the path towards the others, the foal following at its mother's side.

Eight

Mike and the others had seen it all, but they were so shocked that no one spoke and they walked the horses back in silence. By the time they reached the road, Johnny's dad was there with the horse box and they started loading.

The horse box only took four horses at a time and some of the horses weren't easy to get on board. George went off with the first lot.

'We'll leave the mare and foal until last,' he said to Mike. He said nothing to Tess.

As the truck lumbered off down the road, Mike turned to Tess.

'You OK?' he grunted.

Tess had dismounted and was holding Flame's head and stroking her nose. Her hands were shaking.

She nodded. 'I s'pose.' Then, after a pause, 'Did he really mean it, Mike?'

'What?'

'Did you dad mean it when he said I wasn't to come near the horses again?'

Mike shrugged. 'Dunno. Best leave 'im be. It doesn't do to rile him.'

She nodded, twisting Flame's mane in her fingers.

'Why did you come back so soon?'

'Eh?'

'Back from Derbyshire. You weren't there long.'

Mike shrugged. 'Dad's bin offered work abroad.'

'Was there trouble when you left?'

Mike looked up sharply. 'Why d'you say that?'

'I dunno. It was so sudden. Your sister said you weren't due back til Spring.'

'You bin talking to Lizzie?'

'Of course I've been talking to Lizzie. She's my

friend.' Tess rested her head against Flame's neck. 'She said she'd explain to the teachers why I bunked off at break time.'

'You'd best get back.' Mike gestured towards Tess's bike which was lying beside the road. 'I'll deal with the horses.'

Tess shook her head. 'I'll wait till Flame's loaded.'

'Suit yerself.'

They were silent for a while, then Tess said. 'So, what are you going to do?'

'Eh?'

'When your dad's abroad?'

Mike shrugged. 'Mind the horses. Go to the fairs. Work for me uncle.'

'What about the place at Milton, the horse college?'

'What about it?'

Tess didn't reply but continued to lean into Flame's neck, warming her cheek on the mare's shaggy winter coat.

'Me dad says no college can teach me more than he can,' said Mike.

Still Tess said nothing. Mike's anger flared.

'What? You think I'm some no-good gypsy boy that'll never get no job and end up in jail, is that it?'

Tess's head shot up. 'You *know* I don't think that. You know I'm always sticking up for you and your family. I'm always fighting your corner against Ben and his friends … '

'Huh! Ben!' Mike spat on the ground. 'Your brother Ben's the worst of the lot.'

'What do you mean?'

Mike rounded on her. 'D'you know why I gave up on school?'

She shook her head.

'It's because of your brother, that's why. Whenever he gets the chance he taunts us – and I'd just had enough of him and his mates.'

Tess looked shocked. 'So it's not that you don't want to learn? It's because of the grief they give you?'

Mike shrugged. 'Mostly. It happens all the time, day after day. And it gets to you in the end. You think *why bother, what's the point?*'

'Didn't the teachers say anything?'

'Nah. They don't see it.'

'What do you mean?'

Mike looked away. 'Ask your precious brother,' he muttered.

Tess frowned, but she didn't say any more.

She and Mike waited until all the other horses,

except Flame and her foal, had been taken back to the site.

George was driving the empty horsebox when it arrived for them.

Flame was nervous and they had trouble loading her. Several times she got halfway up the ramp and then jumped sideways off it.

In the end, George turned to Tess. 'You try leading her up, girl,' he grunted.

Silently, Tess came up to the mare and patted her neck, then she took the lead rope and started up the ramp, stopping whenever Flame hesitated, talking to her all the time. The foal jumped onto the ramp behind them and suddenly Flame relaxed and walked quietly forward, as the foal gave one final leap into the box beside her and Mike and George pushed up the ramp and bolted it in place.

Tess let herself out of the little door at the other end of the horsebox and picked up her bike. George was standing awkwardly beside her.

'You did well with the mare, girl,' he said at last.

'Thanks,' said Tess, blushing.

'And you're right,' he said. 'She's a rare jumper.'

When they got back to the site, Mike and his dad

unloaded Flame and her foal and walked them round to the field at the back. Johnny's dad and several other men were working on the fencing when they arrived. George nodded at them but said nothing. Mike sensed that there had already been harsh words exchanged.

As they opened the gate to let Flame through, George said, 'Go all round the field, boy. I don't trust the rest of them. Check for anywhere else the horses could push through.'

Mike nodded.

'Useless lot,' muttered George, as he turned to go back to the van.

Mike walked slowly round the field, trying not to put too much weight on his sore ankle. The fencing was old and some of the posts rotting, but the men had done what they could to secure it, sinking new posts here and there and tightening the wire. When he'd been all round and was back at the gate, he stood still for a moment, looking at the horses and smiling to himself.

How he had missed them! He was like his dad. He couldn't live without them. He walked slowly back, not keen to face the family. He'd heard Dad tell his mam on the phone about the new job and he knew she didn't want him to go.

When he went into the day room, his mam was standing in front of the telly, her arms folded. She didn't say anything. She didn't have to. The expression on her face said it all.

But the young 'uns were there and they broke the silence, rushing at Mike, hanging onto his legs, all laughing and talking at once.

George went out, slamming the door behind him.

The kids sat back down on the floor and went back to watching their programme. Mam sat down heavily on the couch and patted the space beside her.

'Come and tell me all about it, love,' she said.

Mike told her about the scrap yard, the filthy, relentless work, Uncle Lash and Aunt Lil. He said nothing about Bret.

'You pleased to be back, then?'

Mike nodded. 'I'm gonna care for the horses, do the fairs and that, when Dad's away.'

'So you're giving up on school, then?'

Mike hesitated. 'Dad wants me to help Johnny's dad too. Earn some money.'

Mum sighed. 'I know.' Her eyes flicked briefly up to the TV screen. 'I'd hoped one of you would be a scholar.'

'Lizzie might stay on at school.'

His mum shook her head. 'Yer dad's set against it. Doesn't want her getting into bad ways, seeing gorger boys and that. And anyway, if yer dad's away working abroad, she'll have to stay back and mind the little 'uns while I'm out cleaning.'

'How did you manage when we were up North then?'

Mum looked at her hands. Mike noticed how rough and worn they were. Mum was only thirty-five. Her hands were those of a much older woman.

'I worked nights, cleaning offices. Didn't do any daytime jobs. But I can't keep that up, Mike. I have to sleep some time.'

'Have you told Lizzie?'

'Not yet. She's set on staying, but you know what your dad's like. His word's law round here.'

'He shouldn't stop her, Mam. Not if she wants to stay.'

His mum sighed. 'I know. But what can I do? He's made up his mind.'

She heaved herself up off the couch and went into the little kitchen to make tea. Mike followed her in, crowding her.

'They'll send the inspectors,' he said.

His mum shrugged. 'What can they do?' she said. 'They'll give us a few books and say she's being home schooled. Then they'll give up.'

Mike stood at the entrance to the kitchen and watched her make the tea.

'Did Dad tell you what happened with Flame and her foal?'

'He said sommat about the foal breaking through onto the railway line.'

'Did he tell you that the gorger girl saved them?'

His mum spun round. 'Tess? What was she doing there?'

'She bunked off school and she got them off the line, Mam. They'd have been killed otherwise.'

His mum put her hand on her heart. 'Lord save us, Mike. What if Tess had been killed?'

Nine

Later that night, Mike was getting into his bed in the shed at the back of their plot. His dad and some of the other men had built two sheds out the back, one for him and one for Lizzie, to give them a bit of privacy. The little 'uns still slept in with his mam and dad in the van.

Mike loved his room, his own territory away from the noise and hustle and bustle of family life.

There was a knock on the door and, without

waiting for an answer, his dad came in. He sat down heavily on the edge of Mike's bed.

'Yer mam and I've bin talking,' he said.

Mike could tell he'd calmed down, was less angry about the horses straying.

'Yeah?'

George frowned. 'Yer mam thinks you should go to this place at Milton.'

Mike couldn't believe it. He didn't answer for a moment. He knew he'd have to choose his words really carefully. He didn't want to blow it.

'If I got a qualification, Dad, a piece of paper, I could work anywhere.'

'What d'you mean?'

Mike swallowed. 'I wouldn't have to work for family. I could work on a big place – a horse stud or a training yard.'

'But what could they teach you, eh?'

'About thoroughbreds, racing, breeding. Even show jumping.' Mike's fists were clenched. 'You've taught me about *our* horses, Dad, about the cobs and the trotting and bareback riding. But I want to learn more.'

'Would you need exams to go to this place?'

Mike nodded. 'I'd have to get a couple of GCSEs, I guess.'

'So you'd want to go back to that school, then?'

'I know what you're going to say, Dad. And I could manage both. I could look after the horses and do a bit of gardening work on the weekends.'

George frowned. 'It's a lot to take on, son.'

Mike took a deep breath. 'Tess would help me with the horses,' he said.

There was a heavy silence.

'She's not one of us, boy.'

'I know she's not, Dad. But look what she did today.'

George nodded. 'She's a natural horsewoman, I'll give her that. And Johnny let slip she'd fair nagged him about the fencing. I suppose that wasn't her fault.'

Mike pressed on. 'Flame's foal will be weaned soon. We could sell it with the others at the next fair, then Tess and the riding school woman could train up Flame properly.'

'As a jumper?'

'Yeah. Then we could sell her as a show jumper.'

'Could make a fair bit on her, I suppose. If the mare's any good. But I don't want no one breeding from her. Another foal would kill her.'

George heaved himself off the bed.

'I'll think about it,' he said as he went out, closing the door softly behind him.

Mike couldn't sleep. He lay in his bed, his hands clasped behind his head, thinking. This was the longest chat he'd ever had with his dad. George was a man of few words and Mike had never been one for talking, either. Chatting was women's stuff. But now he'd said it out loud, he knew this was what he wanted. He didn't want to be like his dad, doing a bit of this and that, relying on family to find a job. He wanted to have a real skill. He knew he had a way with horses – and his dad knew, too.

But if Dad agreed he could try for Milton, then he'd have to go back to school and take exams and he'd have to face Ben and his gang, put up with the taunts.

He unclasped his hands and balled his fists. Horses weren't the only thing his dad had taught him. He'd taught him to fight. He knew he could beat Ben in a fight if it came to it. That wasn't the problem. It was what would happen afterwards. Who would get the blame.

When it came to blame, it was always the gypsy's fault.

The next morning, Mike slept in late and when he got up his dad had gone out. His mum was in the kitchenette and the little 'uns were running around outside, waving sticks in pretend fights.

Mam saw him and smiled. 'Yer dad says you can go back to school if you want.'

For a moment, Mike hesitated. He could hardly believe that his dad had agreed. But did he really want this? In the cold light of day it seemed so difficult. He'd have to go and see the school, talk to teachers, find out about the courses at Milton and what exams he had to pass to get in. And he'd have to do it on his own. No one else would help him.

Then he smiled. He'd manage. Somehow he'd manage.

'Did Dad say Tess could help with the horses again?'

Mam nodded. 'She's a good girl, is Tess.'

Mike said nothing, but later that day, he phoned Tess.

'Thanks for yesterday,' he began.

'How's your dad? Is he still angry at me?'

'No. He says you can go on helping with the horses. And train up Flame once her foal's weaned.'

'Hey, that's SO good! Flame's going to be brilliant, Mike, I know she is.'

Mike smiled at her enthusiasm.

'And he says I can try for a place at Milton and all, if I want.'

'Really?'

'Yeah, only, I'm not sure … '

Tess picked up on the uncertainty in his voice.

'Mr Hardy would help you, Mike. He'd help you fill in forms, talk to teachers and stuff.'

'Yeah. Well. Maybe.'

Mike hummed as he walked down the lane to visit the horses. It was a cold day with a biting wind coming down from the north. He climbed over the gate and went round each of them, looking for any injuries, any signs of ill health. When he came towards Flame, she trotted away from him at first, but he stood still, warming his hands in his pockets, until she came up to him, blowing nervously, the foal, curious, by her side.

He looked at her carefully. She seemed OK after her fright yesterday. She was so different from the others. He'd been with his dad when they'd bought her last year and he'd been surprised, then, that he'd gone for her.

At last she let him stroke her neck.

'You going to jump for us, then, girl?'

She snorted and Mike laughed. Then his phone rang and he dug in his pocket for it.

It was a number he didn't recognise.

'Is that Mike?'

'Yeah.'

He recognised the voice and suddenly everything about the day that had been good, turned bad.

'Bret here. I want you to do me a little favour.'

How does he know my number?

Mike didn't answer. He switched off his phone and put it back in his pocket. His hands were sweating.

A little favour. What did that mean? And if he didn't do Bret a favour, then what? Would Bret tell Lash about the trouble he'd been in before he went up north?

No, it would be worse than that, wouldn't it? If Bret had been rumbled, he'd tell Lash that Mike had been in on the scam, too?

What would happen then? Would Lash be so angry that he'd report Mike to the police? Even though he was family. Report him for being with Bret when he did his thieving.

Mike looked up into the wintery sky. He should have told his dad, told Lash, right away, the first time it happened.

His phone vibrated in his pocket. A text. Sighing, Mike pulled his phone out of his pocket.

From Bret again. Just a name. The name of the guy who'd got them into trouble last year. The guy who conned him and Johnny into thieving.

That was it, then. Bret must know him, and that was how he had his number. He'd change his number, then. Get a new phone.

But the threat wouldn't go away. Bret would make sure of that.

Mike swore out loud, shouting at the sky.

One of the horses shied, startled by the noise.

Mike looked at it – a sturdy brown and white cob with a long heavy mane and a mass of feathery hair over its hooves. Mike's face softened.

'No, boy,' he said 'I'm not going to let that bastard ruin my life.'

Ten

A couple of months later, and there had been some changes. George was working in Europe and Mike was in charge of the horses. He was also helping his uncle with the gardening business at weekends.

And he'd gone back to school. He'd been to see Mr Hardy, who had helped him settle back. It had been really hard at first and several times he'd wanted to give up the school work.

'I've missed so much,' he moaned. 'I'll never catch up.'

But his teachers encouraged him and his mam was that proud of him, too.

'You're a good lad,' she said, as she watched him struggling over his homework. 'I wish I could help you.'

Mike looked up. He could see she was worn out. She'd always had to work hard, his mum – and she had had no schooling. Since the age of eight she'd worked in the fields. She'd often talked about it. She and her family had lived in the fens and, unlike his dad's family, they'd not moved about.

'There was always that much work in the fens,' she'd say. 'Work for the whole family. In the summer we were in the fields from dawn til dusk. We never had no time for schooling. It were a hard life but we were happy. We had all the family round us and we never went short.'

'You couldn't do that now,' Mike had replied.

'Nah. The school inspectors would be down on us. But they didn't bother us in them days,' said his mam. 'They just let us be.'

Another thing that had changed since he'd returned to school was that Ben and his mates didn't get to him so much. They still whispered about him sometimes and gave him death looks, but the insults weren't so obvious and there was less shoving and pushing at break times.

Mike said to Tess, when they were looking over the horses one evening, 'Did you say sommat to your mum, about Ben and me?'

Tess looked embarrassed. 'Yeah. Well, I told her you'd been getting grief from him and his mates.' She paused. 'I guess she said something to him.'

Mike grunted. He was grateful to the gorger girl and her mum for pitching in, but it hurt his pride to rely on women to come to his rescue.

He changed the subject. 'It's the first horse fair next month. We'll sell Flame's foal then.'

'Can I come with you?'

Mike rubbed his chin. 'Me dad wouldn't like it.'

'But your dad's not here, is he?'

Mike shrugged. 'It's all the same to me,' he said. 'But what about your mum? She won't want you rubbing shoulders with a whole crowd of gypsies, will she?'

Tess grinned. 'I'll work on her,' she said.

'Good luck with that,' muttered Mike, wondering what Ben would have to say about it.

They set off for the horse fair very early on a bright

Spring day in May. Tess and Mike had loaded the horses into a huge horse box which took eight horses in all, included Flame and her foal. Johnny's dad drove it and another of the men drove a truck pulling one of the caravans.

Johnny came too, to help, though he was less interested in the horses these days and much more interested in cars and engines.

'What did you say to your mum?' asked Mike, when they were on their way.

Tess grinned. 'I told her we were taking Flame's foal to be sold.'

'That all? Nothing about the fair, or spending the night there?'

Tess squirmed. 'I'll phone her later.'

Mike frowned.

It was a long journey. Although they were mostly on motorways, the horsebox couldn't travel fast and it took them over three hours to reach Stow, stopping only the once for a brew, in a lay-by.

As they reached the town, there was a further delay while they found a place for the box and the caravan and unloaded the horses.

Mike watched Tess's face as she stared about her and, for a moment, he saw it through her eyes. The huge long track in the field, with stalls on either side, and the horses being shown off along the track, trotting at breakneck speed, pulling the trotting carts, young men and boys racing bareback, and everywhere deals being struck, money changing hands, noise and laughter and the smell of food being cooked.

He grinned. It was great. These were his folk. This was where he belonged.

Although Tess hung around, she didn't get in the way. Occasionally she would hold a horse if asked, or go and fetch a hot drink from a stall. Mike and Johnny and Johnny's dad were kept busy the whole day, coupling up the horses to the trotting cart to show off their paces, riding them bareback, shaking hands on a deal.

There was a lot of interest in Flame and her foal. Several folk made an offer for Flame and there was one guy who kept coming back. Each time he offered a bit more money for her, but each time, Mike shook his head.

'She's not for sale,' he said. 'Just her foal.'

He turned to Tess after the man had gone away again. 'There's a fair bit of interest in her.'

'If your dad was here, would he sell her?' asked Tess.

Mike shook his head. 'Nah. He wants to see

what you make of her. You and your riding school friend.'

'You sure?'

'Yeah. 'Course I am.' He grinned. 'We'll get a better price for her if you bring her on.'

By late afternoon, the buying and selling frenzy had died down and the horses were tied up to the horse box, cropping the grass. Mike and Johnny wandered off to look at the stalls and Tess tagged along.

There were gypsy folk everywhere. Groups of young men, girls in glittering gear with fancy hair styles, older men gossiping.

The track was muddy, now, with the constant traffic of hooves and cart wheels, and the mud was trailed into the tented stalls that lined it. Stalls selling all sorts. There were saddles and bridles and harnesses and other horse gear, but there was a whole lot of other stuff, too. China ornaments, CDs of other horse fairs, fancy clothes, hats, boots, rugs, cooking implements and a fortune-telling tent. Mike saw Tess looking at it.

'Want to know yer future, Tess?'

She shook her head.

'Our Lizzie can do it. The palm-reading and that. Our Little Nan could, too,' said Mike.

They passed a woman sitting by some cages with cockerels in them.

'What are they for?' asked Tess.

'Fighting,' said Mike. Tess's eyes widened but she didn't say anything.

'There's proper fighting going on over there,' said Mike, pointing to a circle of men behind the stalls, and without seeing whether Tess would follow, he walked over to join the onlookers.

Two men were stripped to the waist, fists held up in front of them, going at each other, while the crowd cheered them on. Mike and Johnny joined in the cheering but Mike noticed Tess slip away and go to look at some of the painted wagons lined up further back, away from the main track.

He sighed and moved away from the fight. He'd better not leave her on her own.

He caught her up. 'Grand, ain't they?' he said.

'They're beautiful,' said Tess. 'Look at all that decoration. And the chimney coming out the top.'

Mike nodded. Our nan lived in one like that when she was little,' he said. 'She showed me photos.'

Tess nodded. 'Your nan told me they burnt it when her dad died.'

Mike shrugged. 'It was Roma tradition. They're

worth a fair bit now,' he added. 'Folk collect them.'

He saw Tess glance at her watch.

'Have you phoned yer mum, told her yer not coming back tonight?'

She shook her head, took out her phone and walked a little way off. Mike watched her gesturing, explaining. He guessed she'd be in a whole lot of trouble when she got home.

'OK?' he asked, when Tess came back.

'Sort of,' said Tess, switching off her phone and putting it in her pocket.

As it started to get dark, fires were lit by the vans and groups gathered round them, talking, drinking and laughing. Some folk were dancing to the music of an accordion and Johnny's dad picked up two spoons and went over and joined them.

'What's he doing?' asked Tess.

'He's gonna play them,' said Mike.

'The spoons!'

Mike grinned. 'You listen, he'll get a tune out of anything.'

Some families cooked on the open fires, others ate food from the stalls. Tess sat down with Mike and Johnny. Mike looked at her.

'Good, ain't it?' he said.

Tess nodded. 'Everyone's so friendly.'

'We're all family. We all know each other. The fairs are great. It's where we all get together.'

'I wish I had a big family,' said Tess.

At last the party broke up and Mike told Tess where she could sleep.

'You're in the far bunk at the end,' said Mike. 'It's good and private there.'

'Thanks for letting me come.'

'It's bin a good day. And we've done well on the horses, so Dad'll be pleased. Sold Flame's foal for a rare price.'

Mike watched as Tess opened the door to the van and disappeared inside. He leant against the van for a moment, listening to the voices around him, quieter now, and looking out over the dying fires. Then he went and checked the horses.

That's when he saw him.

The man who had conned him and Johnny. He was standing by himself a little way off, staring at their van.

Mike froze and stayed hidden behind one of the horses, in the dark.

Don't let him see me.

But he knew he'd track him down some time. And next time he asked Mike to thieve for him, he'd have a hold over him. He was a friend of Bret's and he'd know Mike had been with Bret when he stole from Uncle Lash. Bret had asked Mike to do him a favour. Mike was sure that the favour had something to do with this guy.

Eleven

Mike was very quiet on the journey home.

'What's the matter, boy?' said Johnny's dad, as he changed gear and drove up the slip road onto the motorway, the gold in his ears and round his neck glinting in the morning sun. 'Cat got yer tongue?'

Mike smiled weakly. 'Just tired,' he said.

He was still quiet when they finally got back to the site and unloaded Flame and the three new horses they'd bought: three cob mares. Flame was restless, pounding round the field, neighing for her foal.

'Will she be OK?' asked Tess.

Mike nodded. 'They always fret for a day or two, then they settle,' said Mike.

'Poor thing,' said Tess.

Mike shrugged.

Tess looked at him. 'What's the matter, Mike?'

'Nothing.'

'Don't give me that. You've hardly spoken today.'

'It's nothing I can tell you,' he said, turning away.

'Why not?'

Mike kicked out at the muddy ground. ''Cos you're just a kid.'

Tess was tired and her temper flared. 'A kid who's been looking after your horses for you, who saved Flame and her foal.'

Mike put his hands in his pockets. He didn't meet her eye. 'Yeah. It's just … well, I'm in trouble. You wouldn't understand.'

'I'm in trouble, too,' said Tess quietly. 'Mum's furious with me. I'm dreading going home.'

Mike smiled. 'My trouble's a sight worse than that,' he said.

'Have you told your mum or dad?'

Mike shook his head. 'I can't.'

'Why not?'

'Shut it, will you. Leave me be.'

There was an awkward silence, then Tess said, 'I'd better get home and face Mum. I don't know what she'll do. She might stop me coming here for a bit.'

Mike looked up sharply. 'Would she do that?'

Tess nodded. 'She's done it before.'

'But she knows us now.'

'It's not you. It's me. Me not telling her about staying over at the horse fair. But if I'd told her, she wouldn't have let me come.'

After Tess had left, Mike put away the trotting cart, the harnesses and the halters and gave a last look at the horses. The new mares seemed to be settling well and Flame had calmed down and was cropping the grass.

He sighed. Part of him knew that the gorger kid was right. He should tell someone. Either he did what Bret wanted – this so-called *favour*, which probably meant getting involved with that gang again – or he had to tell Uncle Lash about Bret's scam and admit to the trouble he'd been in before.

Mike didn't sleep well that night. He tossed and

turned and worried. And the next day at school he was in trouble for not doing his homework.

The last straw was when Ben came up to him, his face red with anger. It was some time since Ben had challenged him. Since he'd been back at school there had only been glances and whispers.

'What the hell do you think you are doing, taking my sister to some low-life gypsy horse fair?'

Mike stood his ground, his fists clenched. 'She asked to come,' he said quietly. 'I didn't know she'd not told your … '

Ben didn't wait to hear more. He rushed at Mike, hitting him in the chest, punching him wildly, throwing accusations at him. Horrible words, shouting, his whole body full of hate.

They'd never had a proper fight before. But Ben had never been so angry before. And Mike was tired and cross.

Mike had been taught how to fight by his dad. Bare knuckle fighting was what all the men did and he'd started learning as a little lad.

Ben was no match for Mike. Mike responded, laying into him, raining blows on him, on his chest, his face, anywhere he could land a punch. He was blinded by anger and couldn't stop, even when Ben was lying on the ground, his hands over his face, trying to protect himself.

'Stop this at once!' Two teachers were running over. One man and one woman. They grabbed Mike and tried to pull him back, but his blood was up and he fought free of them until the school caretaker arrived, a big burly man, and managed to haul Mike away.

'Head teacher's office, NOW!' said the man.

'*And* you, Ben,' said one of the teachers.

The headteacher saw the boys separately. Ben was in the office for a long time, while Mike sat outside, his head bowed and his arms dangling between his knees.

Everything was going wrong for him. Just when he thought things might get better.

At last the door opened and Ben came out. He didn't look at Mike. The headteacher was behind him.

'Ben?' she said.

'Sorry I called you names,' muttered Ben.

Mike looked up and nodded, then Ben walked away.

'Wait there,' said the head to Mike, and went back into her office. Mike heard her talking on the phone.

A little later, Mike was surprised to see Mr Hardy walking along the corridor towards him.

'Hello Mike,' he said. 'Let's go in together, shall we?'

It was a relief to have Mr Hardy there. He'd always been helpful to Mike, always been on his side. But Mike knew he'd gone too far this time. He shouldn't have fought back so hard, shouldn't have kept hitting Ben when he was down.

What would happen? Would he be expelled? Too bad. He was past caring.

He shuffled into the office in front of Mr Hardy.

The headteacher stood up and gathered some papers from her desk. She checked her watch.

'I have to go to a meeting,' she said. 'You know Mr Hardy, don't you, Mike? I'm going to leave you two together now to talk.'

Mike looked up, surprised. He felt the tension draining out of him as he sat down.

Mr Hardy perched on the desk, his arms folded, one of his legs swinging.

'OK Mike,' he said. 'Let's hear your side of it.'

Slowly, haltingly, Mike told him. Told him about Tess tending the horses, told him about the horse fair and why Ben was so angry and then, suddenly, he found he was telling him other things.

About Bret's scam, about Uncle Lash, about how hard it was to keep up with school work and do all the rest.

Mr Hardy let him talk. He never interrupted. He waited until Mike had finished.

'I can see you've got a lot on your plate, Mike. But it can be sorted out, you know.'

Mike frowned. 'How? I can't tell my dad or my Uncle Lash – and Bret's gonna keep on at me to do bad stuff. He thinks 'cos I was in trouble once I'm just another thieving gypsy.'

Mr Hardy sighed. 'There are good and bad people in every culture, Mike. Bret's not a traveller is he? And he's running a scam. And if he's threatening you, then you need to tell the police. And tell your dad and your uncle. If you don't, this guy Bret will always be able to blackmail you.'

'Blackmail?'

'That's what it is, Mike. From what you say, you did nothing wrong. You just didn't tell your uncle about him.'

'But if I dob him in he'll come after me. Or send some thugs after me.'

Mr Hardy smiled. 'I think you'll find that your family will help you there,' he said slowly.

He understand us.

'And you should tell the police about the other guy and his gang.'

'They know about him,' muttered Mike. 'We told them when we was caught, but nothing happened. He's clever. No one can ever track him down and he's always changing his name.'

Twelve

Mr Hardy was right. It wasn't so difficult, after all, to tell Uncle Lash and his dad. Uncle Lash wasn't as angry as Mike thought he'd be when he finally got up the courage to phone him.

'That Bret,' he said. 'I should never have taken him on. I'll see to him myself, lad.'

'I'm sorry I never told you about him – or about the other trouble,' said Mike.

'Huh! That other bloke. He can't hide for ever. I'll spread the word, son. Sooner or later we'll find him and then he won't mess with the gypsies again, I can promise you that. There's gypsy folk all over the country and we don't take kindly to someone conning a couple of our lads.

Mike told his dad, too, when he phoned to find out what had happened at the horse fair. He was so pleased with the prices they'd got that he hardly commented on the business about Bret. He just said 'I'm glad you told Lash, lad. It were the right thing to do.' But he was soon talking about the horses again.

'What about Flame? Is that gorger girl working on her?'

Mike didn't tell him that Tess had been grounded. Her mum had forbidden her to come to the site until after the end of term.

'Yeah. She's working on her,' he mumbled.

Well, by the time his dad returned from Europe, she would be, wouldn't she?

One evening later that week, Mr Hardy came round to the site. Lizzie fetched Mike from the field and, when he got back to the van, Mr Hardy was sitting on the steps. Mam and the little 'uns were there too.

'I've been talking to your mum about what you need to do if you want to register for the course at Milton,' said Mr Hardy. 'I've brought round some forms and I thought we could go through them together.'

Mike wiped his hands on his jeans and nodded. 'Thanks,' he said.

His mum looked anxious. 'What about paying for it?' she said.

'There's no fee if you go at 16, but there will be expenses; you'll have to buy some equipment.'

'Will that be costly?'

Mr Hardy smiled. 'I've been talking to the people at the college,' he said. 'And I think we can get you a grant to cover it.'

'But,' he went on. 'You need a few GCSEs to get in, Mike. '

Mike nodded again.

'They don't need high grades, but you'll need English and three other subjects at grade D. Do you think you can manage that?'

Mike looked down at the ground. 'I dunno.'

'He works ever so hard,' said his mum.

Mike scowled at her. 'But I've missed out on a lot, haven't I?'

Mr Hardy stood up. 'If you want,' he said

slowly. 'I could give you some extra lessons in the holidays.'

Mike stared at him. 'Would you do that?'

'I'd really like to see you get into the college, Mike. I think you'd make a go of it. And you'd have no problem doing the practical stuff, would you?'

'Nah. I guess I already know a lot about horses.'

'Well then, let's fill in these forms, shall we?'

They went into the van and for the next hour they worked at filling in all the forms. When they'd finished, Mike walked with Mr Hardy to where he had parked his car.

'Thanks for your help,' said Mike. Then he blushed. 'If it weren't for you ... '

And although Mike didn't finish the sentence, Mr Hardy understood.

The Travellers
Four people, one story

Rosemary Hayes lives in Cambridgeshire with her husband and an assortment of animals. She worked for Cambridge University Press and then for some years she ran her own publishing company, Anglia Young Books. Rosemary has written over forty books for children in a variety of genres and for a variety of age groups, many of which have been shortlisted for awards.

Rosemary is also a reader for a well known authors' advisory service and she runs creative writing workshops for both children and adults.

To find out more about Rosemary, visit her website: **www.rosemaryhayes.co.uk**

Follow her on twitter: **@HayesRosemary**

Read her blog at **www.rosemaryhayes.co.uk/wpf**